Phonics Storybook

Ken and His Red Tin Rocket

CARAMEL TREE

Ken has a red tin.
"This is my rocket," says Ken.

Ken sits in his rocket.
"Ready! Get set! Go!" says Ken.

Ooops! The rocket drops.

Bang! The rocket bangs.

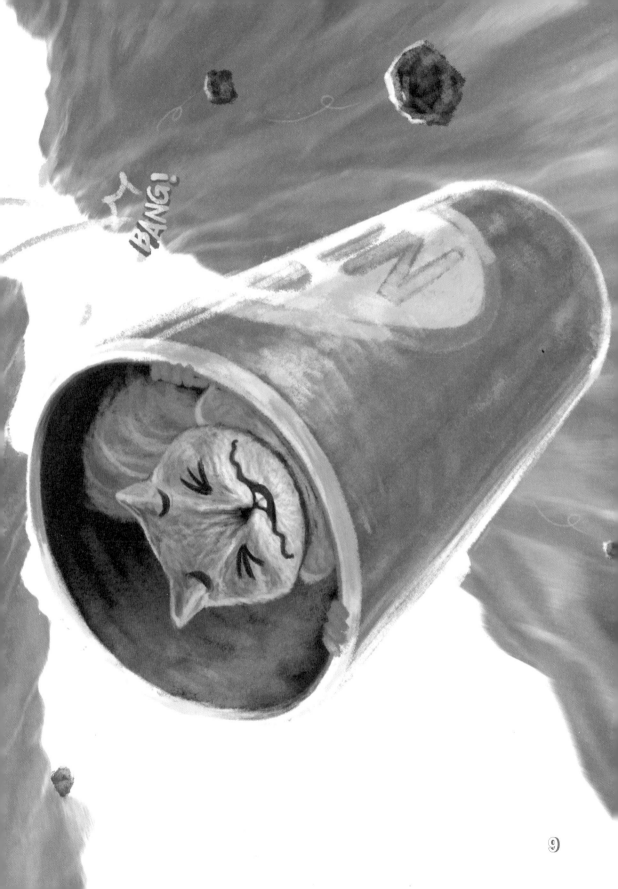

9

Spin! The rocket spins.

"Up!" says Ken.
The rocket jumps up.

Ken opens his eyes.
"Yipee!" he shouts.

Ken is in space.

Ken sees a pink spaceship.

"Hello!" says the robot.
"Hello, hello, hello!" says Ken.

Let's Sing!

Ken and his red tin rocket,
Red tin rocket! (X2)
Ken and his red tin rocket
Ready, get set, go!

Ken and his rocket drop.
Drop, drop, drop! (X2)
Ken and his rocket bang.
Bang, bang, bang! (X2)

Ken and his red tin rocket,
Red tin rocket! (X2)
Ken and his red tin rocket
Ready, get set, go!

Ken and his rocket spin.
Spin, spin, spin! (X2)
Ken and his rocket jump.
Up, up, up! (X2)

Ken and his red tin rocket,
Red tin rocket! (X2)
Ken and his red tin rocket
Ready, get set, go!

has

tin

red

sit

jump

robot

drop

spin

rocket

Short Vowel a e i o u

☐ **Look and learn.**

a

e

has

red

bang

Ken

☐ Look and learn.

i   o   u

tin   drop   up

sit   rocket   jump

Short Vowel a e i o u

○ Look and write.

h a s

dr ⬜ p

r ⬜ cket

t ⬜ n

K ⬜ n

Look and write.

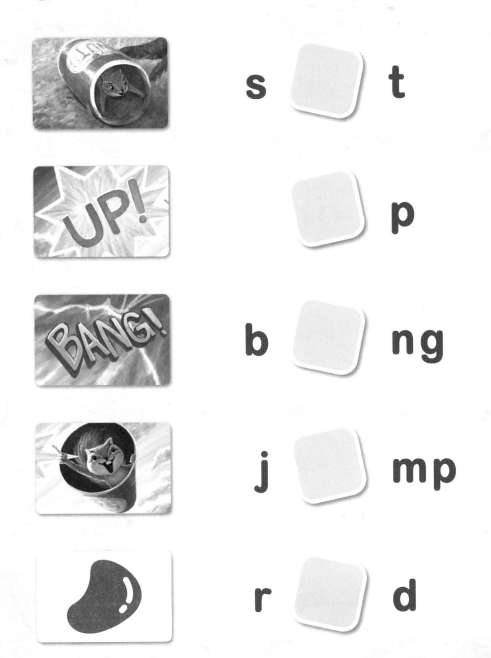

s ☐ t

 ☐ p

b ☐ ng

j ☐ mp

r ☐ d